Jacqueline Wilson

THE SUITCASE KID

adapted for the stage by

VICKY IRELAND

introduced by

JACQUELINE WILSON

NICK HERN BOOKS
London
www.nickhernbooks.co.uk

A Nick Hern Book

The Suitcase Kid first published in Great Britain as a paperback original in 2009 by Nick Hern Books Limited, 14 Larden Road, London W3 7ST

Cover designed by Ned Hoste, 2H

Typeset by Nick Hern Books, London
Printed in the UK by CPI Antony Rowe, Chippenham, Wiltshire

A CIP catalogue record for this book is available from the British Library

ISBN 978 1 84842 013 7

INTRODUCTION

I was thrilled when Vicky Ireland got in touch with me and said she wanted to adapt one of my books for the stage. I immediately warmed to this pocket-sized, dynamic blonde woman. I knew she had a brilliant track record. I knew she understood drama. I knew she had great respect for her child audiences. But when she said she wanted to turn *The Lottie Project* into a play, I thought she was completely bananas. It's a book with a split text, mostly present day, but important parts are Victorian. There are any number of characters, lots of school scenes, street scenes, a seaside setting, a police search including a helicopter, and a huge amusement theme park. How on earth could Vicky conjure this up on stage with a very limited budget and a cast of six?

Well, *I* was the banana. She used her imagination, very clever special effects, evocative music, a brilliant set like a large book and a fantastic cast of actors. I'll never forget that magical first night, sitting amongst so many spellbound children, seeing my imaginary world become a reality on stage.

Since then, Vicky has adapted five more of my books, with ever-increasing success. She certainly had her work cut out adapting *The Suitcase Kid*. The story is in twenty-six sections, one for every letter of the alphabet. The cast includes a tiny toy rabbit called Radish, no bigger than a child's thumb. How was this going to work on stage?

Of course Vicky worked wonders! She wrote her way steadily through the plot, giving the play tremendous verve and pace without sacrificing the alphabet device. There were two very clever versions of Radish. She became so real that many children waved to her at the beginning of the play and gasped in horror when she got lost.

There were a lot of tears shed for poor Andy, torn between her mum and her dad – but there was a smile on everyone's face at the end of the play. I'm sure there'll be tears and laughter when you perform your own version of *The Suitcase Kid*.

JACQUELINE WILSON

PRODUCTION NOTES

Principal Characters

ANDY (*short for Andrea*), *ten years old, large for her age. She is intelligent, sensitive and lonely, struggling with moving each weekend between her respective parental homes. Her constant companion is a small toy rabbit, Radish. Andy is an ugly duckling, waiting to blossom.*

RADISH, *a toy rabbit, much loved by Andy who invests in Radish all the love and care she misses from her own family life.*

MUM, *Andy's mum. Late thirties, attractive and hard-working, doing her best to fit into a new household and be fair to her stepchildren as well as her own daughter. She is a feisty woman in a new relationship, who just wants to enjoy life.*

DAD, *Andy's dad. Late thirties, well-educated and intelligent. He is very much in love with Carrie, his new partner, whilst still being jealous of ex-wife's partner Bill and his household. Although often tired and in financial difficulties, he tries to be responsible and do the right thing by his family.*

CARRIE, *Dad's new partner. Early thirties, pretty, relaxed, outgoing and could be termed a 'hippy'. She has a low income and struggles as a single parent to bring up her twins. She is very tolerant and tries hard to be kind and loving to Andy. She is also heavily pregnant.*

BILL, *Mum's new partner, Andy's stepfather. Late thirties, working-class painter and decorator, has been a widower for some time. He is loud and boisterous, and inclined to be insensitive. He can be both good fun and annoyingly chauvinistic.*

KATIE, *Bill's daughter, Andy's stepsister. Ten years old, small, pretty and spoilt by her father. She is full of insecurities, taking out her fears on Andy, and can be mean and spiteful to those around her.*

GRAHAM, *Bill's son, Andy's stepbrother. Twelve years old, sensitive, thoughtful and kind. He retreats into himself rather than face his father's mockery and his younger sister's demands.*

He is very protective towards Katie because he understands her insecurities.

PAULA, *Bill's daughter, Andy's stepsister. Fourteen years old. Mostly absent, 'doing her own thing'. She has no problems with sharing her home with Andy. (This character could be cut.)*

CRYSTAL, *Carrie's twin son. Five years old, the older twin, clever and thoughtful with a kind and generous streak.*

ZEN, *Carrie's twin son. Five years old, the younger twin, demanding and attention-seeking. A typical noisy five-year-old.*

MRS PETERS, *eighties, kind and generous.*

GREAT AUNT ETHEL, *eighties, loud-mouthed and smells of wee. She only appears at the start of the story and sets the tone of looking down at Andy.*

ZOË, *Carrie and Dad's newborn daughter.*

The Alphabet

The chapters in Jacqueline Wilson's novel are each named after the letters of the alphabet – and all contain words, objects and emotions that reflect each letter. Similarly, I tried to include this device in my adaptation, with an alphabet weaving in and out throughout the play, and important people, places or incidents going from A-Z. The letters and titles of each scene are listed below.

The adaptation sets up the convention of using the alphabet early on. Andy begins the play by discussing with her stepbrother Graham how she will use the alphabet throughout her narration and begins, 'A is for Andy.' Later, she mentions that 'B is for Baboon... and bathroom'. Naming each of the letters in turn fades out after this, but the audiencc should be engaged and encouraged to keep a watch out for the letters themselves. The letters are brought back in more overtly towards the end: X is for Xmas, Y for yacht, Z is for... (and before it's revealed, there's always a passionate whispered response from the children in the audience who already know the story) ...Zoë, the new baby's name.

For the original production, a list of the alphabetical references was included in the programme as a quiz, with the answers given at the back.

Scenes (and corresponding letters of the alphabet)

PROLOGUE

ACT ONE

Scene One	*A is for Andy* The counsellor's room
Scene Two	*B is for Baboon and Bathroom* Mum's home
Scene Three	*C is for Cottage* Mulberry Cottage fantasy
Scene Four	*D is for Dad* Car
Scene Five	*E is for Ethel* Carrie's home
Scene Six	*F is for Friends* Mum's home
Scene Seven	*G is for Garden* Larkspur Lane
Scene Eight	*H is for Haiku* School
Scene Nine	*I is for Ill* Mum's home
Scene Ten	*J is for Jelly* Carrie's home
Scene Eleven	*K is for Katie* Mum's home

ACT TWO

Scene Twelve	*L is for Lake* Larkspur Lane
Scene Thirteen	*M is for Mate, Metal and Meccano* Mum's home
Scene Fourteen	*N is for Night* Mum's home
Scene Fifteen	*O is for Oh!* *P is for Photographs* Carrie's home

Suggested Cuts

The play can be produced in two acts with songs, and will last about one hour and forty-five minutes. Or the script can be cut and performed as one act with no songs, lasting about an hour.

The suggested editing of the play (to create this single-act version) is marked with a thin line running vertically alongside the sections to be cut.

Casting and Doubling

The Suitcase Kid was originally performed by a cast of six adult actors, with the following doubling:
Andy
Mum / Carrie
Dad / Bill
Counsellor / Katie / Crystal / Mrs Peters
Great Aunt Ethel / Graham / Zen / Teacher

With no doubling and large numbers of extras, the cast could be as large as required.

Set Design

The original production of *The Suitcase Kid* was staged in the round, where it is very difficult to have a set design without blocking the view of large sections of the audience. So we used minimal furniture and props which would suggest settings but not be obtrusive or cumbersome. This also had the advantage that the action could move quickly, with scenes flowing easily into each other. A complicated set design really isn't needed (or wanted) for this type of play.

On the floor of the stage area, though, we had a painted floorcloth which had a map showing Andy's journeys. It was based on Nick Sharratt's original illustration, which is on the front cover of this book. Strung around the upper gallery of the theatre, there was a wooden frieze of the letters of the alphabet. At the end of the play, when Andy says, 'It's as easy as A, B, C,' the A, B and C letters lit up.

There are two mulberry trees mentioned in the play. In the original production these were presented in an abstract way by a table and matching chairs that had wooden designs looking like roots, and another couple of chairs held aloft to represent the branches. In Scene Nineteen, all the chairs were positioned together to resemble the gnarled branches of the Larkspur Lane mulberry tree. On the underside of the chairs were small models to represent the furniture that Mr and Mrs Peters place inside the hollowed trunk of the tree. By turning over the chair, each furniture piece was revealed.

When the production moved to a larger proscenium-arch theatre, the backdrop was a large map of Andy's journeys. There were flaps in the side walls used for entrances and through which the two beds could be pushed on and offstage.

Stage Furniture

Six chairs.
A table.
A washbasin on a pedestal with a reversible mirror. One plain side, the other covered with white foam stripes (see Radish Fantasy Two, below).

A small unit containing TV/video set and a collection of videos and DVDs.
Katie's bed and bedclothes.
Andy's bed and bedclothes.
A large rug with Crystal and Zen's assorted toys, books and action figures attached to it, to be easily carried in and out.
A Christmas tree.
A hospital bed and bedding.

Costume Design

The costumes in the original production were all designed with the quick changes of the cast in mind, since they were each playing multiple characters.

Andy wore a green school uniform, Graham a grey school uniform and Katie simply bright day clothes. Carrie wore a wig, a floaty dress and a pad so she would look pregnant. Bill wore dungarees and a woollen hat with long hair attached, and Mrs Peters wore a shawl and a soft beret with grey hair attached.

Music

Music was specially composed for the original production, but it would be possible to find existing music that would be appropriate. Different moods of music should be used to underscore and reflect Andy's complicated world, its mixture of good and bad times, and the many journeys she takes.

In the two-act version of the play, there are a number of songs incorporated into the action. The lyrics of these are included in the text that follows, though you may choose to cut them from your production.

When staging your own production, Steven Markwick's original music may also be licensed for performance. It is available for hire by schools and amateur groups in two forms: 1) a piano/vocal score for all the songs plus some incidental music; 2) a CD of the backing tracks to the songs for use when live piano accompaniment is not available. Please apply to the Performing Rights Manager at Nick Hern Books, details on page iv of this book.

Puppets

In the original production, I decided to present the characters of Zen and Crystal as puppets to give them the small stature of five-year-olds. They were very simple to operate with strings from their arms, legs and head, attached to a wooden crossbar. The actors operating them also spoke their lines.

There was also a one-foot-high puppet version of Radish which had jointed limbs and was operated by the actress playing Andy (see further explanation below). A doll was used for newborn baby Zoë.

Staging the Radish Fantasies

There are many occasions in the novel when Andy plays with her little toy rabbit Radish, and during these times she is truly happy and liberated. I decided to try to capture this fleeting happiness and include it in the action of the play, as a counterpoint to the sadness she experiences in her real life.

For the original production a one-foot-high puppet of Radish was created which could easily be seen by the audience. In four fantasy scenes when Radish comes to life, the puppet was animated by the actress playing Andy. Other members of the cast also joined in, wearing appropriate costumes and rabbit ears on their heads, and we had some wonderful music to accompany each scene.

1. *Radish's New Home* (*page 3*)
The cast entered as rabbit removal men carrying small items of furniture for Radish's new home in the mulberry tree in Larkspur Lane. This echoes what happens at the end of the play, but I used it as a prologue to start the action. It worked particularly well at the Orange Tree Theatre which has an intimate, wooden auditorium with an upstairs gallery not unlike a large embracing tree.

2. *Radish's Snow Adventure* (*page 11*)
Andy started this scene by squirting Bill's shaving-foam canister to resemble snow falling, then as the lights went out, the cast entered with white ribbon sticks which they twirled under UV

lights so the stage transformed into a magical snowy world of white shapes. They created mountains and valleys which the puppet Radish joyfully danced and slid along. Then, as they exited and the lights returned, we saw that the bathroom mirror (rotated in the darkness) was now covered in white streaks, indicating the havoc Andy's reverie had wrought.

3. *Radish's Wedding* (*page 21*)
Radish entered wearing a wedding veil and carrying a bouquet. The cast assembled around her as excited and happy wedding guests posing for photographs. Radish then threw her bouquet as she exited and the guests rushed offstage after her.

4. *Radish's Tarzan Experience* (*page 31*)
The cast created a jungle scene from bits of material, flowers and fans, plus lots of jungle noises. Radish swung from creepers around the stage, escaped an alligator and slid down a waterfall before she exited in triumph.

This play is dedicated with my love and admiration to Jacqueline Wilson, Sam Walters and everyone involved in the original production, plus huge thanks to the Orange Tree Theatre, and Chris and Elizabeth of Watershed Productions.

VICKY IRELAND

The Suitcase Kid was commissioned by and first performed as a one-act play in-the-round at The Orange Tree Theatre, Richmond, London on 22 August 2007, then toured by Watershed Productions throughout the UK, including a two-act proscenium-arch run at Warwick Arts Centre over Christmas 2007. The cast was as follows:

ANDY	Sarah-Lee Dicks
MUM / CARRIE	Holli Hoffman
DAD / BILL	Henry Everett
KATIE / CRYSTAL	Kerry Gooderson
GRAHAM / ZEN	Mostyn James
UNDERSTUDIES /	Matt Houlihan
ASSISTANT STAGE MANAGERS	Abigail Lumb
	Elizabeth Rowden

Director Vicky Ireland
Designer Pip Leckenby
Lighting Designer John Harris
Music and Lyrics Steven Markwick
Puppet-maker and Advisor Lee Threadgold
Choreographer Ben Redfern

FOR THE ORANGE TREE THEATRE, RICHMOND, LONDON
Artistic Director Sam Walters
Administrative Director Gillian Thorpe

FOR WATERSHED PRODUCTIONS
Executive Producer Chris Wallis
Producer and General Manager Elizabeth Jones

THE SUITCASE KID

Characters *(in order of appearance)*

ANDY, *short for Andrea*
MUM (CAROL), *Andy's mum*
DAD (SIMON), *Andy's dad*
GREAT AUNT ETHEL, *Andy's great aunt*
FAMILY COUNSELLOR
BILL, *Mum's new partner*
KATIE, *Andy's stepsister, Bill's daughter*
GRAHAM, *Andy's stepbrother, Bill's son*
PAULA, *Andy's stepsister, Bill's older daughter*
CARRIE, *Dad's new partner*
ZEN, *Andy's stepbrother, Carrie's twin son*
CRYSTAL, *Andy's stepsister, Carrie's twin daughter*
TEACHER, *at Andy's school*
HEADMISTRESS, *at Andy's school*
MRS PETERS, *an old lady*
BABY ZOË, *Andy's new baby stepsister, Carrie and Dad's daughter*

Note

Suggested editing of the play (to create a shorter, single-act version) is marked with a thin line running vertically alongside the sections to be cut.

Prologue

Music. Enter ANDY *with the puppet Radish. She beckons the rest of the* COMPANY *onstage for the 'Radish's New Home' fantasy (see Production Notes, page xii). They enter dressed as removal men who wear hats with rabbit ears. They show small pieces of furniture to Radish, who points and directs where she wishes each piece to be placed around the stage.*

The actress playing MUM *is* RABBIT 1, *'Thumper'. The actor playing* DAD *is* RABBIT 2, *'Warren'. The actress playing* KATIE *is* RABBIT 3, *'Bugs'. The actor playing* GRAHAM *is* RABBIT 4, *'Roger'.*

RABBIT 1. Here we are, Radish!!

RABBIT 2. Good morning, Radish! My goodness, what a magnificent mulberry tree. It's going to make a splendid home for you. The team's all here to move you in. My name's Warren, I'm the boss. Come on, lads! Hop to it!!

RABBIT 1 (*holding up item*). One red lamp. Where's your sitting room, Radish? (*Exits.*)

RABBIT 3 (*carrying box*). My name's Bugs. Where's your kitchen? (*Exits.*)

RABBIT 4 (*carrying box*). Right, Radish, couple of bits for the bedroom. Got a wardrobe here and a bed. What am I doing with these, Radish? Up on that branch there? Lovely. Thumper, mate, I'm coming up to the bedroom. (*Exits.*)

RABBIT 3 (*carrying box*). Right, Roger 'ere. I've got a kitchen stove and a kitchen table. Put 'em in those roots over there, shall I? Perfect. (*Exits.*)

RABBIT 2 (*carrying items*). One sink, one bath. Where's your bathroom, Radish? Up there in that branch? Smashing.

RABBIT 1 (*enters*). 'Ere, Warren, isn't it time for our tea break?

RABBIT 2 (*as he exits*). Put the kettle on, Thumper.

RABBIT 3 (*enters*). Right, Radish. Why don't you come and see where we've put everything…

RABBIT 3 *exits with the puppet Radish.*

Eventually, ANDY *and* GRAHAM *are left onstage, as the music and the fantasy fade.*

ACT ONE

Scene One

A is for Andy

ANDY *and* GRAHAM *sit side by side on the table, centre stage.*

There are four chairs around the table. ANDY *holds the Radish doll.*

ANDY. How did it happen? It wasn't Radish's fault. She didn't mean to fall into the hole in the tree, it was a mistake. But then what a wonderful thing it turned out to be. Her own little home in the tree…

GRAHAM. That's not the beginning.

ANDY. So?

GRAHAM. So, you should start at the beginning.

ANDY. Which is?

GRAHAM. 'A'. And go through it all like the alphabet. You said it was like that.

ANDY. I didn't.

GRAHAM. You did.

ANDY. Well, it was.

GRAHAM. Right, then.

ANDY. You're mad.

GRAHAM. I don't care. Do it properly. Make us guess.

ANDY. What?

GRAHAM. The letters of the alphabet, Dopey.

ANDY. All right. We'll start with the obvious. 'A.' A is for Andy. I'm Andy and this is Graham, my stepbrother, who is a real pain, but anyway…

ANDY *and* GRAHAM *exchange smiles.* GRAHAM *changes onstage into* GREAT AUNT ETHEL.

DAD *and* MUM *enter holding a baby, made from* ANDY*'s school coat.*

I was a large baby.

Enter GREAT AUNT ETHEL.

When she first saw me, Great Auntie Ethel, who smelt of wee-wee and shouted, said –

GREAT AUNT ETHEL. What a great big child. Is she really yours? I think she's a cuckoo. Well, let's hope she's got brains, 'cos she certainly hasn't got beauty.

GREAT AUNT ETHEL *exits.*

ANDY. Thank you, Great Auntie Ethel. (*She takes the coat from* MUM *and puts it on.*) Well, I've got brains, lots of them, but I'm still really big for my age and I know I'm not very pretty. And I do have this problem with my family. Follow me.

COUNSELLOR, MUM *and* DAD *sit at the table.* ANDY *joins them.*

COUNSELLOR *opens her bag and takes out two dolls which she places on the table.*

COUNSELLOR. You can play with them if you like. That's a Mummy doll, and that's a Daddy doll.

ANDY. No, thanks. I don't really like dolls.

COUNSELLOR (*to* MUM *and* DAD). Well, do make yourselves comfortable.

ANDY *takes the Radish doll from her pocket and nuzzles it.*

Oh, how sweet. What's Bunny's name?

MUM. Radish. Andrea's had her for years and years. She's a very important member of our family.

DAD. I bought her as a Saturday treat for Andy. I like to give her little things now and then.

MUM. You didn't. I gave Radish to Andrea when she was about three, in her Christmas stocking.

DAD. You didn't.

MUM. I most certainly did.

DAD. What?!

COUNSELLOR. Never mind. The fact is, she's very important. Hello, Radish. I expect you're feeling a bit sad and worried about where you're going to live now. We know what Mummy wants and we know what Daddy wants, but what do you want, eh? (*Pause.*) I think she's a bit shy. Maybe it's hard to talk in front of so many people. (*To* MUM *and* DAD.) Would you mind stepping outside for a few moments? I'd be most grateful.

DAD. Oh, righto.

MUM. Of course.

They exit.

COUNSELLOR. Poor Radish. It's a bit tough on her, isn't it?

We hear MUM *and* DAD *arguing outside.*

COUNSELLOR *moves the dolls.*

Well, here's Mummy and here's Daddy. Let's build them each a house, shall we? (*She does so with toy bricks from her bag.*) There. Now, Andrea, does Radish want to live in House A, with Mummy, or House B, with Daddy?

ANDY. Neither.

COUNSELLOR. Oh. Well, where does she want to live, then?

ANDY. In House C with both of them.

MUM *and* DAD *are shouting offstage.*

COUNSELLOR. Yes, I know she does, but she can't. Not any more. Your mum and dad just aren't happy living together, you know that. But they both love you very much and they want you to be happy, so which house do you think Radish would like to live in? House A? Or House B?

ANDY. House C. But if she can't – and I still think she can – then she wants to live in House A *and* House B.

COUNSELLOR. Ah. You mean she wants to live in House A one week and House B the next? As easy as A, B, C.

COUNSELLOR *exits.*

ANDY. So that's what happened. Well, not quite. Radish still lives in my pocket like she's always done but now I live with Mum one week and Dad the next. It's as easy as A, B, C – I don't think.

GRAHAM *enters and hands her a suitcase.*

Scene Two

B is for Baboon and Bathroom

ANDY. This is my new family at Mum's house.

Music. Characters pass across the stage as they are introduced and also set furniture, including two beds, two chairs and a bathroom sink.

BILL *enters.*

That's Mum's new man, Bill the Baboon. My un-Uncle Bill. I can't stand him. He's all hairy and squashed up. I've never seen his bottom but I bet it's red like a baboon's. He's a painter and decorator. Came to do the hall at Mulberry Cottage when Dad moved out. That's how he met Mum.

PAULA *enters with headphones, crosses and exits.*

That's my older stepsister, Paula. She's hardly ever here. She's okay but she hates Mum – cool. If they fight enough, we might leave.

GRAHAM *enters.*

This is Graham who is seriously brainy. He's okay but never speaks. Well, he didn't then. His dad bullies him and talks down to him just because he's clever, which is really out of order…

KATIE *enters.*

BILL (*to* GRAHAM). Come on, brainbox…

BILL *and* GRAHAM *take the table offstage.*

ANDY. And that is Katie. Same age as me – yes, really! You think she looks sweet? Like a little sugar mousey? Well, she's not. She is a king-sized *rat.*

Music fades.

KATIE*'s room.*

KATIE. Oh, not you again. You're so big you really get in the way. This is my room, remember, but as we have to share, I say where you can put things.

ANDY *drops her coat.* KATIE *kicks it.*

Not there.

She draws a line across the room with her foot.

Song – 'Never Cross This Line'

KATIE.

From the ceiling to the floor, this is my room,
From the window to the door, this is my room,
And if you're gonna stay here,
There's one thing you better know... oh oh oh –
This is
My room –
And don't you forget it.
My room –
Or else you'll regret it.
My room –
So don't ever let it slip through your mind:
NEVER CROSS THIS LINE.

Don't touch my books or my CDs,
Don't wear my clothes or my jewellery,
'Cos everything you see here
It all belongs to me... yeah yeah yeah –
This is
My room –
So don't rearrange it.
My room –
'Cos nothing's gonna change it.
My room –
Just follow this golden rule and we'll be fine.

KATIE / ANDY.

My / Your room –

KATIE.

And don't you forget it.

KATIE / ANDY.

My / Your room –

KATIE.

Or else you'll regret it.

KATIE / ANDY.

My / Your room –

KATIE.

So don't ever let it slip through your mind:

KATIE / ANDY.

NEVER CROSS THIS LINE.

KATIE.
It's mine, mine, all mine,

KATIE / ANDY.
NEVER CROSS THIS LINE.

KATIE.
It's a crime, crime, crime, crime,

KATIE / ANDY.
NEVER CROSS THIS LINE.

KATIE.
Do I have to say it one more time?

KATIE.
Never cross this –

ANDY.
Never cross this –

KATIE.
NEVER CROSS THIS LINE!

And you can't put anything here, on the windowsill, so. (*She picks up picture in frame.*) This is my mother. She's dead. She was extremely beautiful and I take after her. I have unusual colouring.

ANDY. How old were you when she died?

KATIE. Dunno. Can't remember. Right. We're supposed to be watching a film, so I'll choose. (*She looks through the DVDs.*)

ANDY. What've you got? (*She stretches to see over the line.*) *Watch With Mother*? My mum and dad used to watch that with me when I was little.

KATIE. I'll put it on if you want. (*She puts on the DVD. We hear it playing.*) I've never seen it, it's for babies. I've got lots of Walt Disney's and some great films my dad doesn't know about. I keep them in my *Teletubbies* cases. They're all blood and really, really violent… Oh, look at that puppet. I don't believe it. He's called Andy Pandy like you.

ANDY. I'm not. I'm just called Andy.

KATIE. No. You're Andy Pandy like him – 'cos you're both stupid.

ANDY. Get lost.

KATIE. Andy, Andy, Andy-Andy Pandy!

ANDY. Shut up. Stop it.

KATIE. Shan't. Andy, Andy, Andy-Andy Pandy! – Oh, look, he's getting into his basket with Teddy. (*Sings.*) 'Time to go home – time to go home' – Oh dear, Andy Pandy, you can't go home, can you, 'cos you haven't got a home to go to. How sad is that…

KATIE *and* ANDY *fight.*

(*Screams.*) You're over the line!!

ANDY. So what, Ratface?

MUM *enters.*

MUM. Stop it, Andrea! How dare you hit Katie? You're twice her size. Don't be such a bully. I am so ashamed of you. Katie's gone out of her way to welcome you into her home and you behave like this!

ANDY. It's not fair, you don't know what she's like.

MUM. I don't care.

KATIE. She hurt my arm, Auntie Carol.

MUM (*to* KATIE). Did she, sweetheart? Well, it's all right now, so you go and get yourself a drink, eh?

MUM *tidies the room.*

ANDY (*whispering to* KATIE). I hate you.

KATIE (*whispering to* ANDY). Why don't you get in your basket?

KATIE *exits.*

ANDY *throws herself on her bed.* MUM *sits next to her.*

MUM. Now, what on earth was all that about?

ANDY. She called me names.

MUM. What?

ANDY. Andy Pandy.

MUM (*laughing*). That's not so awful.

ANDY. Yes it is. It's from that television programme.

MUM. Yes, I know. Well, Andy Pandy's okay. He's the hero. I suppose he's a bit wet, but you're not. Why don't you call her Looby Loo and tease her back? But don't fight. I won't have it.

ANDY. You don't understand.

MUM. Oh, mums never understand. Come on, cheer up. (*She hugs* ANDY.) Why don't you read for a bit? That always makes you feel better.

ANDY. 'Cos I don't know where any of my books are. They were all shoved away in a cardboard box. Anyway, it's so noisy I can't concentrate. Katie puts the telly on all the time, and she hides all my stuff and scribbles on my homework. I hate it. There's nowhere to be on my own any more.

MUM. Oh, come on, it's not that bad –

We hear the front door slam.

That's Bill. Better get the tea started.

MUM *exits. We hear* MUM *and* BILL *greet each other offstage.*

ANDY. B is for Baboon… and bathroom. (*Shouting off.*) Well, I'm locking myself in the bathroom if you're at all interested. At least I can be on my own in there. (*She goes into the bathroom and sits. She sees hairs on floor.*) Ugh. There are Baboon hairs everywhere. Right, I'm going to do a spell with all these little bits you've left, Mr Hairy Bum. I hereby brew this spell so Bill the Baboon will fall off his ladder tomorrow and break his hairy neck. Bet he doesn't. (*She sees shaving cream.*) Shaving cream!! What's that, Radish, you want to play snowmen? Yes! Okay – here we go. (*She sprays foam.*) A snow rabbit and a snow cottage and it's snowing more and more and more –

Music.

'Radish's Snow Adventure' fantasy (see Production Notes, page xii).

BILL *enters.*

BILL. Hurry up in there!

Fantasy and music end.

ANDY. Whoops. Oh dear, the Baboon needs a pee. Sorry. (*She leaves the bathroom.*)

BILL. About time too – I'm bursting. What's that smell? My shaving cream?? (*He enters the bathroom.*) What the…?! CAROL!! Have you seen what she's done in here?

MUM, KATIE *and* GRAHAM *enter.*

MUM. Oh, Andrea!! What have you done??

KATIE. In trouble again, are we, Andy Pandy? You're sooo stupid.

ANDY. I was only playing…

All exit except ANDY.

It wasn't always like this. I had a really nice life once with my mum and dad. We lived in the most beautiful place on earth.

Music.

Mulberry Cottage.

Scene Three

C is for Cottage

MUM *and* DAD *enter with puppet of little* ANDY. *They walk across the stage.*

MUM. Come on, Andy.

DAD *hides behind a suitcase.*

DAD. Who's hiding behind the mulberry tree?

They start to exit. DAD *lifts and twirls puppet* ANDY.

MUM. Oh, Simon, you spoil her!!

They kiss and exit with the puppet.

ANDY. It was so lovely, just the three of us. But that was ages ago. Now, it's Friday.

Music fades.

Time to change homes.

Scene Four

D is for Dad

ANDY. Time to go to Dad's for the week. He lives with Carrie and her twins –

Zen and Crystal. He hardly ever comes inside any more since he had a fight with the Baboon. It was horrible. They were really hitting each other, and Mum was yelling and I tried to stop them, but they wouldn't listen. I thought they were going to kill each other. Then squeaky little Katie came in and said, 'Oh, please, Daddy, you're scaring me,' and they stopped, just like that. The little rat.

ANDY *collects her suitcase and joins* DAD *in the car, which is made from two chairs.*

DAD. Hi, darling.

ANDY. Hi, Dad.

We hear the sound of a car setting off and travelling.

I had another fight with Katie today.

DAD. Who won?

ANDY. I did.

DAD. Good for you. She is one spoilt child.

ANDY. Uncle Bill says *I'm* spoilt. I only complained 'cos I didn't get the Coco Pops again. Said I had to share. Well, I've never had to share before. He really told me off.

DAD. Cheek.

ANDY. Yes, he was horrible.

DAD. Well, if he does that again or anything like that, you phone me right away, okay? It's crazy having to live with them when you'd be much happier living with me all the time, wouldn't you?

ANDY. Mm.

DAD. I really miss you when you're at your mum's place.

ANDY. I miss you too.

They arrive. The car sound-effects fade.

DAD. Here we are. We're quite early, you know. How's about an ice cream, just you and me? No need to tell Carrie.

ANDY. She'd make me eat carrot sticks.

DAD. How about *two* ice creams? One strawberry, one chocolate?

ANDY. Wow! – Well, um, as there's lots of time, maybe we could do something else instead?

DAD. Instead of ice creams? Okay, what do you want to do?

ANDY. Go to Mulberry Cottage?

DAD. Oh, Andy, don't start.

ANDY. I'm not. I just want to go to Mulberry Cottage, one last time, please, Dad?

DAD. What's the point? We're never going back there. There's another family living there now.

ANDY. I know. I just want to see it, that's all. And the mulberries might be ripe and we could pick some and Mum could make one of her pies and we could all eat it together for tea and –

DAD. Stop it, Andrea. You're being silly. It can never be like it used to be, you know that. Just let it go.

Scene Five

E is for Ethel

DAD *and* ANDY *get out of the car.* CARRIE *greets them.*

DAD. Here we are.

CARRIE. Hi, Andy. Come on in. (*She kisses* ANDY.)

ANDY. Hi, Carrie.

The TWINS *enter.*

CARRIE. Lovely to see you. You look really well. Andy's here, twins. Sorry about the mess. Just push your way through. That's it. (*She picks up a futon.*) Look, I've a surprise for you.

ANDY. What is it?

CARRIE. It's a Japanese futon.

ANDY. A what-on?

CARRIE. Futon. It's a sort of sleeping bag, and look, I've done little embroideries all over it, see?

ANDY. Oh, wow, yes. It's great. Thank you, Carrie.

CARRIE. I thought it would be really useful for when you come to stay. Your very own bed.

ANDY. Yes, for me.

CARRIE. And for the twins' friends when they stay too.

ANDY. Oh. Yes, but it'll hurt my neck being tied up in a bag all night long.

DAD. No, it won't. It's lovely. Don't be such a whinge, Andy.

CARRIE. I'll fetch you a pillow. Where did we put the pillows, Simon?

DAD *and* CARRIE *exit.*

ANDY. And my back, lying on the hard floor in that thing… Where's the mattress?

ZEN. Whingey-pingey.

CRYSTAL. You can share with me if you like, Andy.

ANDY. No, thanks. You wet the bed.

CRYSTAL. Only sometimes.

ANDY. Sorry. Look, I need some space for my things, and this bag has to go somewhere.

She throws things around. CRYSTAL *laughs.* ZEN *gets angry.*

ZEN. Stop it. You're mucking up my Transformers. (*He kicks* ANDY.)

ANDY. Owh!

She trips him up. He punches her in the stomach.

CRYSTAL. Don't, Zen. You mustn't hit people in the tummy, Carrie said.

ZEN. She said I mustn't hit *her* in the tummy because of the baby. I can hit other people though.

ANDY. Oh no you can't. What's all this about a baby?

CRYSTAL (*sucking her thumb*). Shiz gone have a bebi.

ANDY. Take your thumb out of your mouth.

CRYSTAL. It's Carrie and Simon's baby.

ZEN *kicks* ANDY.

ANDY. Stop that, Zen, you silly little squirt.

They fight. ANDY *sits on* ZEN.

DAD *and* CARRIE *enter.*

DAD. What's going on? Andy, get off Zen, he's just a little kid. What are you doing?

CRYSTAL. Actually, Simon, Zen was actually kicking her quite hard.

DAD. That's no excuse.

ANDY (*to* CARRIE). You're going to have a baby.

CARRIE. That's right. Isn't it lovely?

ANDY. But you've got Zen and Crystal. What do you want more children for?

CARRIE. Well, I want Simon's child, too.

DAD. We were going to tell you this weekend, honestly.

ANDY. It doesn't matter. I'm not interested. I don't like babies.

DAD. Oh, come on. I think you'd love a baby sister.

ANDY. No, thanks. Anyway, how do you know it's going to be a girl? It could be a boy. A boy like Zen. *Twin* Zens!

CARRIE. No, I had a scan, in case it was twins again, and it's just one baby. A little girl.

Pause. CARRIE *hugs* ANDY.

What shall we call her, Andy? Your little sister?

DAD. Yes. How about you choose a name for her?

ANDY. Okay. (*To herself.*) The worst name possible? A name for someone who'll smell of wee-wee and shout a lot? (*To the others.*) I think she should be called Ethel.

CARRIE. Oh. (*Pause.*) I know, let's have some tea.

All exit. ANDY *is left on her own, feeling wretched.*

Scene Six

F is for Friends

GRAHAM *enters.*

GRAHAM. Don't stop. Keep going.

ANDY. I don't want to.

GRAHAM. Go on. I'm listening.

ANDY. All right.

GRAHAM *exits.*

It's getting awful in my two homes and there's nobody much to tell about it. My best friend Aileen stopped being my best friend when I left Mulberry Cottage. She plays with Fiona now after school 'cos they still live near each other. I get left out. I come home from school by myself now. Both journeys. They said it would be easy.

MUM, KATIE *and* GRAHAM *assemble on one side of the stage.*

MUM. All you have to do is leave school, walk down Seymour Road, round Larkspur Lane and up Victoria Street into town, take the 29 from the bus station as far as The Cricketers Pub, then walk the rest of the way – about ten minutes. I'd meet you, you know that, but I don't finish work until five, and they won't let me off any earlier. Anyway, you'll be fine, I'm sure you will...

ANDY *swings round.* DAD *is on the other side of the stage.*

DAD. All you do is get a 62 from the bus station, then a 144 and walk the rest of the way, about fifteen minutes. Easy peasy, lemon squeezy.

DAD *exits.*

ANDY. They don't realise how tired I get. And how worried. All sorts of things happen. (*To* MUM.) I lost my bus fare today and an old lady had to pay for me. It was awful. Really embarrassing.

MUM. Oh dear.

MUM *takes money from her purse and gives it to* ANDY.

There we are. You can give it back to the lady tomorrow. Poor Andy. I hate you having to come home by yourself but there's nothing I can do.

KATIE. *I've* been coming home by myself since I was six years old, Auntie Carol.

ANDY. That doesn't count. Your stupid school is just down the road. A baby could crawl there.

MUM. You know, I wish you'd swap to Katie's school. It'd be so much more sensible.

KATIE. Yes. And you wouldn't have to wear that terrible school uniform. Mr Brown in the sweet shop calls Andy 'the jolly green giant'.

GRAHAM. Only 'cos her coat's green.

ANDY. No. It's 'cos I'm not little and cute like her. He was being size-ist.

MUM. But St Martin's is so much more convenient.

ANDY. Yes, it's okay from *here*, but it would take hours and hours and hours when I'm staying at Dad's.

GRAHAM *and* KATIE *exit.*

MUM. Well, all this to-ing and fro-ing is getting ridiculous. You're worn out. I'm just thinking about you, darling. It would be so much better if you'd settle down in one place and go to the local school.

ANDY. That's what Dad says.

MUM *exits.*

But I like *my* school, even though it's not the same. Even though Aileen's not the same.

Scene Seven

G is for Garden

ANDY. But, one good thing, I've found another mulberry tree – by accident. It's in this garden in Larkspur Lane.

Music.

I was walking home from school one day and I looked up and suddenly – there it was, all old and twisty with loads of fruit on it. Come and see. The garden's really wild. No one about.

She goes to the tree, looks around, grabs some fruit, then runs back and eats it.

These are mulberries. They're so good, like a cross between a raspberry and a strawberry but even yummier.

Music fades. ANDY *enters school.*

If you eat too many, you get the runs, but it's worth it. I go there every day now on the way home. Both homes. And sometimes on the way to school too.

Scene Eight

H is for Haiku

ANDY *sits down.*

The TEACHER *enters and talks to an imaginary class.*

TEACHER. Right, class, poetry books open, please, page twenty-three. There's a really interesting example there of a poem from another country…

The TEACHER *now mimes talking to the class.*

ANDY. And Radish loves it in the garden too. She goes on jungle expeditions and crosses rivers and climbs mountains. She is not afraid.

TEACHER. So listen again class and follow the beats.

The ancient pond lies still.
A frog leaps in.
The sudden sound of water.

Which is what, Andrea?

ANDY. Er…

TEACHER. It is a haiku – And a haiku is?

ANDY. When you kick someone?

TEACHER. No, that is kung fu. I will say it again. A haiku is a short Japanese poem, with exactly seventeen beats. Listen and this time, concentrate… (*He mouths a silent poem.*)

ANDY (*to herself*). A short Japanese poem with seventeen beats?

The frog went boing, boing, boing,
Zoooooom, splat.
Fancy that.
He missed the water.

Sixteen beats.

In my dreams,
I am as small as my rabbit,
And I am safe at home.

Seventeen beats! I did one!!

I like haikus a lot.

(*To* TEACHER.) Sorry, sir.

HEADMISTRESS *enters.*

TEACHER (*as he exits*). Headmistress.

HEADMISTRESS (*to* ANDY). No, stay where you are, please. (*To other imaginary children.*) You may run along. (*She watches them leave then turns to* ANDY.) Now, Andrea, it's just not good enough. Your schoolwork has gone to pieces. Your homework is either late or you just don't bother to do it. You keep forgetting your PE kit and you don't bring a proper sick note when you're ill. Now, what's going on, eh? You must try harder, do you understand?

ANDY. Yes, Mrs Davies.

HEADMISTRESS. Then see you do.

HEADMISTRESS *exits.*

ANDY.
I live with Mum.
I live with Dad.
I live with Radish.
Can't we join up?

Scene Nine

I is for Ill

ANDY. It's Friday morning. Nearly time to go to Dad's.

I feel ill.

Mum's home.

ANDY *lies on bed.*

Mum! Mum!!

MUM (*off*). What's the matter?

ANDY. MUM!

MUM (*off*). Coming.

MUM *enters. She is late for work and flustered.*

ANDY. I feel hot and my head hurts.

MUM. Poor lamb. Let me feel. (*She feels* ANDY*'s forehead.*) Goodness, you are hot! You're burning up. I think you've got flu. Well, you certainly can't do that awful journey to school, not in this state. You'd better stay in bed.

ANDY. By myself?

MUM. Maybe I should stay at home too.

ANDY. Oh, Mum, would you?

MUM. Well, they won't like it, but I can't see what else we can do. You're really not well, are you? You'd better stay in bed this weekend.

ANDY. What, at Dad's?

MUM. No, here. You're in no fit state to travel. I'll ring work and then I'll get you a nice cold drink. Come on, back into bed. That's it. Snuggle up.

MUM *exits.* KATIE *enters.*

KATIE. Staying in bed, are we? Poor little weakling. Well, if you touch any of my stuff while I'm at school, I'll get you. I'll put your precious Radish head first down the loo. Poo-ee! And then she'll have to be dunked in a bowl of disinfectant to get her clean and she'll smell disgusting for days and days and days and days and...

MUM *enters with a glass of water.*

MUM. Go on, Katie, or you'll be late.

KATIE *exits.* MUM *sits and reads a newspaper.*

ANDY *drinks the water. She plays with the Radish doll.*

ANDY. Mum? Can I have your lace hanky? (ANDY *takes it and winds it round Radish's head.*) Thanks. There, look. Radish is a bride.

Music.

*'Radish's Wedding' fantasy (**see Production Notes, page xiii**).*

Music fades.

I feel a bit better now.

MUM (*looking at her watch*). It's almost teatime. What do you fancy?

ANDY. Jelly.

We hear a car horn.

It's Dad, come to collect me. (*She starts to get up.*)

MUM. Stay right where you are.

MUM *exits. An argument between* MUM *and* DAD *is heard off-stage.* KATIE *enters.*

KATIE. Oh no! I've been at school all day and I come home and you are still in bed! Poor Andy Pandy. Have your legs dropped off yet?

DAD *enters.*

DAD. Hi, Andy. Well, you seem fine to me. You've just got a bit of a cold, but everyone's got the sniffles at the moment. Come on, get dressed and we'll get cracking.

DAD *starts to pack* ANDY*'s suitcase.* ANDY *gets out of bed.* MUM *enters.*

MUM. Don't be stupid, Simon, you can't take her out into the cold air when she's got flu. Get back into bed this instant, Andrea.

MUM *starts to unpack.*

DAD. Oh, for heaven's sake!

ANDY *cries.* MUM *and* DAD *wrestle with* ANDY*'s suitcase.*

KATIE. I don't feel very well, either, Auntie Carol. I think I've got Andy's flu.

MUM. Of course you haven't. Don't be ridiculous.

KATIE. I might have.

KATIE *exits.*

DAD. Well, is she coming with me or not?

MUM. No. Why are you being so stupid?

DAD. Don't call me stupid.

DAD *starts to exit with* ANDY.

ANDY. Daddy, I haven't got my shoes on…

MUM. She's staying here!!

MUM *takes the suitcase, puts it by the bed then exits.* DAD *hovers.* ANDY *moves across the stage to* DAD*'s. She unpacks.*

Scene Ten

J is for Jelly

ANDY. So I stayed in bed all weekend, then I went to Dad's. But on Friday morning, I still felt odd.

She tries to hug DAD.

DAD. No. I've got to get to work and you've got to get to school. You were play-acting last week. No, no cuddles.

ANDY. But I feel funny, Dad. I really do. It's so cold in this flat.

DAD. Zen and Crystal don't think so.

ANDY. That's 'cos they wear their pyjamas under their clothes. I have to wear two pairs of everything. Everything!! I just can't get warm.

DAD. All right, I'll turn the storage heaters up.

ANDY. That won't do any good. I don't know what they store but it's certainly not heat.

DAD *exits*. ANDY *gets into her sleeping bag*.

I'm getting in my bag. Got to get warm. Put the heat on. Put the futon on. Put the heat on the futon, on… I feel seriously weird.

ANDY *falls asleep. Music. Nightmare sequence:*

CARRIE *enters. She has a huge baby attached to her that she manipulates and makes crying sounds*. ANDY *wakes up*.

ANDY. Oh, the baby's here, and it's huge…

DAD *enters and speaks in a melodramatic voice*.

DAD. No! It cries when you get near it, so stay away, further away.

ANDY *struggles in her bag*.

Why are you crying? You're not setting your little sister Andrea a very good example.

ANDY. What do you mean, 'Andrea'? *I'm* Andrea. You said I could name the new baby. She's Ethel. I'm calling her Ethel.

DAD. Don't be silly. You're not Andrea. She's my little girl now and she's called Andrea.

ANDY. No!! *I'm* your little girl. *I'm* Andy. Agh!!

The baby and DAD *exit.*

ZEN *and* CRYSTAL *enter. Music fades.*

Lights up. ANDY *wakes up.* ZEN *is sitting on her.*

ZEN. Wake up.

CRYSTAL. You were shouting. Were you having a bad dream?

ANDY. Yes. Get off me.

CRYSTAL. Get off her, Zen. I don't think you're very well, Andy.

ANDY. I don't think so either. (*She cries.*)

CRYSTAL. I'll get Carrie. Carrie!

ANDY. No, I want my dad.

CRYSTAL. Simon!!

DAD *and* CARRIE *enter.*

CARRIE. Poor little fruitcake. It's Friday. Friday always makes you feel bad, doesn't it? Would you like me to show you some of the relaxation exercises we do at childbirth classes? They really help you stop feeling tense.

CARRIE *demonstrates pre-natal breathing exercises.*

DAD. She's not tense. She's got a fever, feel.

ANDY. My throat hurts. And my head, and my neck, and my arms, and my legs. You said I was pretending but I'm not. Oh, Dad, will you stay at home and look after me?

DAD. You poor old sausage. All right, no school. But Carrie will have to look after you. I can't stay off work.

ANDY. But I want you, Dad.

DAD. Don't be silly.

ANDY. Please.

DAD. All right, just this once. I'll ring the office. Say my little girl needs me.

CARRIE. Good. That's sorted. Now, Andy, what would you say to a big bowl of my bean casserole?

ANDY. No, thanks.

CARRIE. But it's very nutritious.

ANDY. My throat's too sore.

CARRIE. Oh dear. Well, is there anything else I can get you? What do you really fancy?

ANDY. Jelly.

CARRIE. Jelly? All right. I'll make you a lovely orange jelly for tea. I'll have to buy some oranges. I've never made a jelly before but I think it'll turn out all right.

ANDY. Well, all you do is pour boiling water on the stuff and stir it.

CARRIE. Oh, that's jelly out of a packet. I'd never give you junk food, Andy. You need natural, fresh food with lots of nourishment. Yes. It won't take long.

Time passes. DAD *mops* ANDY*'s brow. The* TWINS *play quietly.*

CARRIE *returns with jelly in a bowl, and a spoon.*

Here we are. Wibble-wobble, wibble-wobble. There. (*She gives* ANDY *the bowl and spoon.*) I'll just tidy up a bit. Rather a lot of washing-up to do.

CARRIE *exits.* ANDY *stares at the bowl.*

DAD. Come on, Andy, eat up. Carrie made it for you specially.

ANDY. I'm not hungry.

DAD. What's the matter?

ANDY. Why is it brown? It's supposed to be orange. And it isn't jelly. (*She bangs it with her spoon.*) It's like concrete. It's seriously disgusting.

DAD. Don't be silly. You've got to eat something.

ANDY. I feel sick.

DAD. Now, don't start.

ZEN. I'll eat it.

CRYSTAL. No, you can't, it's for Andy.

ZEN. I don't care. I want it.

DAD. Oh, do be quiet, Zen.

ZEN. Carrie, I want jelly too.

CRYSTAL. You are a baby. *I* don't want jelly.

ZEN. Jelly-belly Andy.

MUM (*calling from off*). Hello? Is anyone here?

DAD. Oh no, it's your mother. I'd better go and sort her out.

DAD *exits with* ZEN *on his back.* CRYSTAL *follows.*

CRYSTAL. Simon, I want a piggyback.

MUM *and* DAD *confront each other offstage.*

MUM (*off*). Where's Andy?

DAD (*off*). Ill. She's in bed.

MUM (*off*). What do you mean, 'She's in bed'? For heaven's sake, I can't believe it! I didn't think even you could stoop so low. Just because Andrea was genuinely ill the other weekend –

DAD (*off*). Well, she's ill again.

MUM (*off*). Oh, of course she's not ill. You're just being deliberately obstructive! Come on, hand her over this minute.

DAD (*off*). The child is very ill. She's got a sore throat and a fever –

MUM (*off*). I'm not surprised, stuck in this disgusting, damp basement, it's no place for young children –

DAD (*off*). Well, if you hadn't bled me dry over the divorce we might be able to afford a better place –

MUM (*off*). Andrea? Andrea, darling? It's Mummy. I've come to take you home.

MUM *enters.* DAD *follows.*

Poor lamb! Get your coat. You're coming home with me this instant.

ANDY *gets up and steps in the jelly.*

ANDY. Er –

MUM. Oh my goodness! *What's that?*

ANDY. Jelly. Carrie made it for me.

MUM. Jelly! That stupid hippy's been feeding you that muck and calling it *jelly*?

DAD. Will you stop calling Carrie names?

MUM. I'll call her what I like! She's never looking after my daughter again, do you hear? I'm sending the Social Services round. Suitcase, Andrea!

ANDY *picks up her suitcase and she and* MUM *go home.*

DAD *exits sadly.*

Scene Eleven

K is for Katie

MUM. You are never going back there. He can ring and come round and write all the letters he wants. It won't do any good.

ANDY *gets into bed.* MUM *exits in tears.*

ANDY (*speaking from under the bedclothes*). Oh, Radish. Do you have a sore throat too? Well, the only cure would be a sip of magical mulberry juice –

KATIE *enters, hears* ANDY *mumbling and silently mimics what she is saying.*

– so we must search high and low across barren lands, but our throats remain sorely parched. Still, we must journey onwards, always seeking the path. Always seeking the magical way... Are you all right, Radish?

Pause.

KATIE. No!!

ANDY *emerges from under bedclothes, embarrassed.*

I don't believe it. You are such a loser! So what's the matter this time, poor ickle invalid? Why don't you just shove off back to your boring old dad. I'm sick of you cluttering up my bedroom. Your mum's not serious about you being here always, is she?

ANDY. I don't know.

KATIE *puts on the Andy Pandy DVD.*

Oh, ha-ha, very funny. Switch it off!

KATIE. No. It's time to get into your basket, Andy Pandy. Did you get that? Just fold up your great, huge, horrible arms and legs, and stuff your fat head into your basket, right, and I'll post you off to your dad. Only, once the new baby is born, there won't be room for you there either so you'll just have to stay stuffed up in your basket for ever, okay, because nobody wants you.

ANDY. They do want me, so there. My mum wants me *and* my dad... That's what all the fuss is about.

KATIE. No they don't. They only go on about you because they want to get at each other. If they really wanted you, they'd have stayed in that boring old cottage you keep going on about. But your dad left 'cos he wants his new lady, and your mum left 'cos she wants my dad. Not you. Got it?

ANDY. Shut *up*!

They fight noisily. MUM *enters.*

MUM. Whatever's the matter now? (*She turns the DVD off.*)

KATIE. Andy's poked me in the eye and it *hurts*!

ANDY. I didn't!

MUM. Andrea, I've told you to stop all this nonsense. I won't have you bullying Katie. Come here, sweetheart, let's see. Your eye's all right now.

KATIE. It hurts.

MUM. Yes, well, it is a bit red. Andrea, how *could* you?

ANDY. I didn't touch her stupid eye. I didn't. I didn't!

MUM. Come on, we'll bathe it.

MUM *and* KATIE *exit. We hear their voices off.* ANDY *cries.*

BILL *enters.*

BILL. What a commotion. Yes, well, I'm glad to see you're feeling sorry, Andrea. Dear, oh dear, you little girls! And I thought it would be smashing for you both, being the same age and that. I know it's difficult with Wonder Boy Graham hanging around, and Paula – well, she's hardly ever here – but listen to me, Andrea. I know you've had a hard time and you're not very well, but that's still no excuse. You must stop hitting my Katie or you'll really hurt her. She's only small, my Katie. She's not used to rough and tumble. She's been a good little girl sharing her bedroom with you and all her precious bits and bobs –

KATIE *enters and hovers with a wet cloth over her eye.*

– so I'd like you to try and be a bit more grateful. I know you're a nice kid underneath, even though you've got a bit of a temper on you. Got that from your dad, obviously. But you've got to learn to control yourself, all right?

KATIE. My eye still hurts, Daddy.

BILL. Does it? Oh, my poor little princess. I'm going to get you a huge box of choccies, and then you can have a cuddle with yer old dad, eh?

KATIE. Yes. (*She sticks her tongue out at* ANDY.)

BILL. Come on, then. (*He turns back to* ANDY.) And remember what I've said to you, young lady, or you'll be in real trouble.

BILL *and* KATIE *exit.*

ANDY. I wish…

Song – 'A Place of My Own'

ANDY.

A place of my own,
Somewhere I can be
All by myself,
Where no one shouts at me.

Somewhere to go
When I'm feeling down,
A place of my own
With no one else around.

A place of my own
For Radish and me,
A place of my very own.

I don't need the latest phone
Or a computer screen to make me happy,
I just need a place of my own
Where I can sit and dream.

A place of my own,
Where no one bothers me,
A place of my own
Underneath the mulberry tree.

A place of my own
For Radish and me,
A place of my very own.

A place of my own
For Radish and me,
A place of my very own.

Lights and music fade.

End of Act One.

ACT TWO

Scene Twelve

L is for Lake

ANDY. I wish I had a place of my own, with my own things, and my own rabbit. Where she can have some fun. There's a pond in Larkspur Lane, in the old garden. Perhaps we could play there. A boat. Radish could go boating on the lake!! I'll make a raft. Pencils – Sellotape – (*She collects them from various locations and makes a pencil raft.*) Here we are. (*She tries it out in the basin, but it sinks.*) Oh. It's sunk.

Scene Thirteen

M is for Mate, Metal and Meccano

GRAHAM *enters.*

ANDY. Graham, you haven't got a toy boat, have you? I mean, I know you're too old for toys, but did you ever have one?

GRAHAM. I made one from a second-hand Meccano set once.

ANDY. That's really clever. Did it float?

GRAHAM. Course not. It was metal.

ANDY. Well, then it was a pretty stupid boat, wasn't it? What does float? I've tried pencils but they're not right.

GRAHAM. Cork.

ANDY. Cork. You mean, like the top of a bottle? Not big enough. What else?

GRAHAM. Rubber.

ANDY. On the end of a pencil? Far too small. Come on, Graham.

GRAHAM. Plastic.

ANDY. Plastic. Thanks.

GRAHAM *exits.* ANDY *thinks, then gets an idea.*

One of the Baboon's empty cassette cases! (*She finds one and tries it out in the basin.*) Whoops, sunk. Too small. I know – an empty video box!

She looks around then gets one of KATIE*'s video boxes and takes it to the basin. It works.*

Yes! She can go on an adventure holiday. Come on, Radish! Off into the jungle!!

Music.

'Radish's Tarzan Experience' fantasy (see Production Notes, page xiii).

MUM *enters with a chair. Music fades.*

MUM. Just because I told your father you're never going to stay with him again, he says he's going to take me to court. Typical. The mean-minded, egotistical snake. Well, he's not going to win.

DAD *enters with two chairs.*

DAD. Why don't you just let it go?

MUM. No, I've told you, Andrea's never staying with you again.

DAD. Then I intend to get in touch with my solicitor. You've been warned.

MUM. I don't care.

COUNSELLOR *arrives with a chair. They all sit.*

COUNSELLOR. Hello again, Andrea. How's Radish?

MUM. I can't let her stay with her father any more.

DAD. We'll see about that.

MUM. ...It's an appalling situation, all cramped together in that damp, squalid basement, with a mad hippy and two children who never have any clean clothes on.

DAD. Oh, and I suppose your Mr Painter-and-Decorator is perfect? Well, I'm here to tell you he is a hairy ape and his children are spoilt idiots with no manners at all.

MUM. And what do you suppose you are? Behaving like petulant two-year-old –

DAD. And you are a self-opinionated, pompous...

ANDY. I need the loo.

ANDY *exits to listen from the side of the stage.*

COUNSELLOR. How do you think Andrea's coping with all this?

MUM. It's awful for her –

DAD. Yes, really unsettling. But when she's been with me a few days she calms down – and by the end of the week, she's fine.

MUM. That's because she knows she's coming back to me.

DAD. Absolute rubbish. The poor kid's been missing me dreadfully, she says so herself.

COUNSELLOR (*opening a file*). Have you noticed anything different or unusual in her behaviour?

MUM. She's always okay with me.

DAD. We get on like a house on fire. Always have done.

COUNSELLOR. It's just that her school says she's rather withdrawn and isn't doing very well at her lessons.

MUM. What do you mean? She's always been very outgoing. She's got loads of friends.

COUNSELLOR. Yes, of course, but Andrea's had quite a lot to cope with recently. Children in these circumstances often develop worrying little habits which tend to show when they're under stress. They might be a bit whiny and demanding – bite their nails – wet the bed... Sometimes they start stealing, but it's not as serious as it sounds. It's just taking a few things to get a bit of attention.

MUM. Oh, dear. Andrea has started taking a few things recently.

DAD. Well, she's never stolen anything from us. Just shows where she wants to be.

MUM. It's not really stealing. And she takes such silly things –

DAD. Like what?

MUM. Well, I found this pile of things under her bed. Some of my pencils and the Sellotape, one of Bill's cassette cases, and one of Katie's video cases. Empty. It doesn't make sense.

COUNSELLOR. Perhaps she just wants to annoy you all to get some attention?

MUM. She certainly doesn't get on with Katie. They're always fighting.

DAD. She fights with Zen and Crystal too, but if she could be with us for longer I'm sure we'd settle down and be one big happy family, especially when the new baby arrives.

MUM. Sorry, but she needs to be with me. She can't cope with the idea of a new sister, she's told me.

COUNSELLOR. Yet she already has to cope with five ready-made brothers and sisters. You can't expect her to get on with all of them. She doesn't want to be with them. She doesn't want to be with your new partners. She simply wants to be with you two.

ANDY *nods.*

Which of course is not possible. I'll just go and see where she's got to. (*She goes off to the side.*) Ah, there you are, Andrea. Would you like to come back in?

ANDY *does so. Smiles all round.* MUM, DAD *and* COUNSELLOR *exit.*

ANDY. It's no good. They think they understand, but they don't. And the counsellor's wrong. I don't hate all my family. Graham's all right. In fact, he's the best. (ANDY *puts on a dressing gown.*)

GRAHAM *enters from the bathroom in his dressing gown, carrying a small boat.*

GRAHAM. For you. (*He gives* ANDY *the boat.*)

ANDY. Wow!

GRAHAM. This one floats. I've tried it out in the bath. And it'll take one passenger easily.

ANDY. Oh, Graham. (*She hugs him, much to his embarrassment.*) It's lovely. It must have taken you ages. Why did you bother?

GRAHAM. I like the way you keep having a go at Katie. Before you came, she always used to get at me and mess up my stuff, you know – really annoying. But now she gets at you instead. It's cool.

ANDY. Yeah, it's not fair. I can't get away from her. It's rubbish having to share a room. Tell you what, I could come in with you sometimes, couldn't I?

GRAHAM. Er. No. I don't think so. It's too small, what with my computer and everything…

ANDY. Okay. Anyway, I've got my own secret place.

GRAHAM. The bathroom?

ANDY. No, better than the bathroom. I go there after school. It's why I want the boat. Anyway, thanks ever so much, Graham. We're mates now, aren't we?

GRAHAM. If you like.

ANDY. I do and so does Radish. Night night.

GRAHAM. Night.

Scene Fourteen

N is for Night

GRAHAM *sits at the side of stage and reads a book.* ANDY *gets into bed.* KATIE *is watching TV and trying to stay awake. We hear the sound of horror-movie music.*

ANDY. Oh, for heaven's sake, switch that stupid thing *off*!

KATIE. It's my telly and my bedroom. I can do what I want.

ANDY. I'll tell my mum.

KATIE. So? I'll tell my dad.

ANDY. I want to go to sleep.

KATIE. Well, *I* want to stay awake.

ANDY. Look, I'm turning it off, so tough titties.

KATIE. And *I'm* turning it on, so 'tough titties' with knobs on.

ANDY. You're such a baby. I know why you sit up all the time and drink water so you have to go to the loo. It's to keep yourself awake because you're scared of the dark!

KATIE. Oh, scared, am I?

She turns up the volume. ANDY *gets out of bed, takes her pillow and lies down at the side of the stage.*

ANDY. Fine. I'll sleep on the landing, then. See if I care.

GRAHAM. What's up?

ANDY. I can't sleep 'cos that idiot sister of yours has got the telly on all the time.

GRAHAM. I know. I used to share with her, remember? She didn't have a telly then so she used to make up all these games and tell ghost stories, and if I fell asleep she'd hit me with her torch. She really beat me up.

ANDY. I just don't get it. Why doesn't she get tired like normal people?

GRAHAM. She does. Look at the bags under her eyes. And she falls asleep at school.

ANDY. So why won't she go to sleep like everyone else?

GRAHAM. 'Cos she's scared.

ANDY. But she makes herself scared watching all those horrible films.

GRAHAM. No. They're just to keep her awake. She's scared of going to sleep.

ANDY. Why?

GRAHAM. She just is, that's all.

ANDY. Of going to sleep? *Why?*

GRAHAM. Because, when our mother died, they told us she'd gone to sleep. I knew she was ill and I knew when she'd died. But Katie was just a little squirt and she didn't know what 'dead' meant. So they said it was like going to sleep. They were trying to be kind but she got really scared after that. So she'll do anything to stay awake.

ANDY. I see. (*She gets up to go.*)

GRAHAM. Andy?

ANDY. What?

GRAHAM. Don't say anything. I mean, I know she's a pain, and she's my sister and I hate her, but all the same, don't go on about it.

ANDY. All right.

ANDY *returns to the bedroom and gets into bed.*

Katie, why don't you switch that off and come in my bed for a cuddle? What do you think?

KATIE. What on earth makes you think I want to come into your bed, Andy Pandy? You're so big and fat I'd get squashed in five minutes flat.

KATIE *settles down to sleep leaving* ANDY *furious and humiliated.*

Scene Fifteen

O is for Oh!

P is for Photographs

ANDY. OOOOooooooooohhhhhhhh! See if I care. I'm going back to Dad's this week.

ANDY *is packing and moving homes.* KATIE *exits.*

They sent a social worker to check the flat out…

Carrie's home. CARRIE *enters with a washing basket.*

CARRIE. …and the social worker said it was spotless. So please tell your mother that, Andy. We might be a bit untidy down here but the flat is perfectly clean.

The TWINS *enter.*

And she said that Zen and Crystal are delightful and intelligent children.

ANDY. Oh no, I've forgotten my PE kit.

CARRIE. It's all right, I washed it. Here. (*She hands it over to* ANDY.)

ANDY. Oh, thanks. (*She holds up the blouse.*) That's my school blouse?

CARRIE. Yes, I popped it in with Zen's red sweater by mistake.

ANDY. But it's pink!

CARRIE. I know, and it'll look lovely with your green uniform, much better than boring old white.

DAD *enters with a camera. He takes photos.*

Oh, ha-ha. You'll wear that out. I bought that camera for your dad so he can take lots of photos of the baby *actually being born*. As it pops out!! Won't that be lovely?

DAD. And I want to take lots of photos of my number-one daughter too. Come on, Andy, give us a smile. That's it. Great!

CARRIE. Andy, the star model! Come on, let's dress you up.

Music.

CARRIE *dresses* ANDY *with things from the washing basket.*

You look fantastic, Andy. You ought to be a fashion model when you grow up. You're nice and tall already and fashion models have to be tall. There you go. Now, I'll go and run the twin's bath.

CARRIE *exits.* DAD *takes photos and* ANDY *poses. Music fades.*

ANDY. Let's see. Oh no! Delete them, please. I look awful.

DAD (*looking at the photos*). These are great! Well, that one's a bit dark, and you're a bit out of focus there – but on the whole, they're really good. I'll get you some copies if you like.

DAD *hands her photos then exits with the* TWINS.

ANDY. Thanks, Dad.

DAD (*off*). See you next week.

Scene Sixteen

Q is for Questions

MUM *enters.*

ANDY. Look, Mum.

ANDY *shows* MUM *the photos.*

MUM. Oh, for heaven's sake, what have they done to you? You look awful. What are you wearing… those are Carrie's clothes! What were you doing? Why on earth couldn't your father take some proper photos of you instead of all dolled-up like a dog's dinner?

KATIE *and* GRAHAM *enter and look at the photos.*

ANDY. I was being a fashion model, just for a bit of fun. Carrie said I ought to be a model when I grow up – she did, Mum, honestly.

MUM. She would.

KATIE. Fashion models aren't *fat.*

ANDY. I can go on a diet.

GRAHAM *looks at the photos.*

Don't, Graham. I look awful.

KATIE. Yeah, you said it, Andy Pandy.

GRAHAM. I think you look pretty. (*Exits.*)

KATIE. Pretty awful!

MUM *puts the photos away and doesn't notice as* KATIE *takes the Radish doll from* ANDY.

ANDY. Don't you touch her!! Leave her alone!!

ANDY *retrieves the Radish doll and hits out at* KATIE.

MUM. Andrea! I've told you time and time again, you are not to hurt Katie, no matter what she does.

KATIE. I'm gonna tell my dad on you!

MUM. Come on, Katie, we'll go and bake a cake for tea. (*To* ANDY.) What's the matter with you? I wish you'd grow up.

KATIE *and* MUM *exit.*

ANDY. Come on, Radish. We'll escape. We'll go to Larkspur Lane. (*She sets off walking.*) We don't need cake.

Music.

DAD *enters.*

DAD. Andy.

ANDY. Yes, Dad?

DAD (*reading from a letter*). This letter's from your headmistress. She's moaning about your dental appointments, saying they should be after school, but as far as I know you haven't had any dental appointments. Have you? Have you, Andy? Have you?

DAD *exits as* HEADMISTRESS *enters.*

HEADMISTRESS. Andrea!

ANDY. Mrs Davies…

HEADMISTRESS. You're daydreaming again. For goodness' sake, girl, you must stop this silly habit. I know things have been difficult for you at home, but lots of parents divorce and move house. It's very upsetting, but it's not the end of the world. Well, Andrea. What do you say? Speak up…

COUNSELLOR *enters.*

COUNSELLOR. Hello again, Andrea.

ANDY. Oh no.

COUNSELLOR. Do you mind going from House A to House B to House A to House B to House A to House –

ANDY. Yeeeeeeeeeeees! I just want to be left alone. I hate school but I can't bunk off, and I hate home. I haven't got a home. Neither has Radish. She's so tired of living in my pocket.

ANDY *keeps walking.*

Scene Seventeen

R is for Radish

ANDY *arrives at the mulberry tree and plays with the Radish doll until the music fades. It is now dark.*

ANDY. Radish, don't fall asleep. We can't stay too long. Everyone keeps asking me questions when I just want to be left alone. It's just not fair.

Song – 'A Place of My Own' Reprise

ANDY.

A place of my own,
Somewhere I can be
All by myself,
Where no one shouts at me.

A place of my own
For Radish and me,
A place of my very own.

Music fades.

I wish we could stay here in the garden for ever. But it's getting dark. I daren't stay any more. Mum'll be cross I missed tea, and the Baboon will have a go at me, and Katie will start saying horrible things. I just hate it all.

ANDY *cries. Music. A torchlight comes on. A figure appears, creating a giant shadow.* ANDY *leaps up.*

I'm so sorry! I know I shouldn't be in your garden. I'm leaving now.

Ohh – Radish, Radish – where are you? Radish!

ANDY *panics and runs. The light goes off and the figure exits.*

MUM, BILL, KATIE *and* GRAHAM *enter, calling for* ANDY.

Music fades. Lights snap up.

Everyone crowds round ANDY *in her bedroom.*

MUM. Oh, thank goodness. Where on earth have you been?

ANDY. I was just… playing.

MUM. What!! (*Shakes her.*) Oh, Andy, I'm sorry. (*Hugs her.*) But do you know what time it is? I was so worried when you went off like that – Oh, darling, never mind that. All that matters is you're safe.

ANDY. But Radish isn't. I've lost her.

BILL. For goodness' sake, is that why she's so late? Because of a toy?

ANDY. She's *not* a toy, she's a mascot.

BILL. Hey, hey! No need to take that tone. Look, your poor mum's been worried sick. You've been gone hours, young lady. It's just not good enough.

MUM. Yes, I know, Bill, but Radish is very special to Andy.

BILL. All the same, it seems a bit daft, the whole family going demented just because she's lost a rabbit that's not even real.

ANDY. She's real to me.

MUM. Come on, now, calm down. You are being a bit of a baby, you know?

ANDY *pulls away.*

Now, don't be like that. Maybe we can find Radish.

ANDY. She fell inside a tree.

KATIE. Which tree?

ANDY. And I've lost the boat.

GRAHAM. It's all right. I can make another one.

BILL. And I'll get you another rabbit in the morning. They sell them in the toy shop down the road. Katie had some of those… erm…

KATIE. Sylvanian…

BILL. Sylvanian wotsit Family thingies when she was little.

ANDY. I don't want another wotsit thingy. I want *Radish*. I've got to go and comfort her –

BILL. What's she on about?

MUM. Don't be silly, darling. You're going straight to bed. Come on. And don't ever do that again, promise?

MUM *kisses* ANDY *goodnight.* MUM *and* GRAHAM *exit.*

Song – 'Unexpected Turns'

BILL.

Life can take some unexpected turns,
Suddenly you're heading down a different path,
When you're not looking it will come and find you,
Sneak up behind you just to have a laugh.

Some good, some bad,
Some happy, some sad,
Life can take some unexpected turns.

I am not an educated fella,
All that I could tell ya could fit on one page.
Life has taught me if you try and plan it,
You're a silly gannet not a clever sage…
…and onion…
Have a banana…

As a wise man once said,
Before he lost his head,
Life can take some unexpected turns,
Life can take some unexpected turns,
Life can take some unexpected turns.

BILL *exits.*

KATIE. Down a tree, is she, Andy Pandy, with all the bugs and spiders, eh? Maybe some bird has fallen down the hole and died and your little Radish is lying on its corpse. Yeah, with all the maggots and beetles going wiggle-wiggle-wiggle all over her and she won't be able to cry for help because rabbits can't talk. She's just opening her mouth and screaming silently, wondering why you don't come.

ANDY *gets out of bed and puts her pillow under the covers to create a human shape.*

What are you doing?

ANDY. What do you *think* I'm doing? I'm going to find her.

KATIE. But it's night-time. You can't go out.

ANDY. Just watch me.

KATIE. But your mum said –

ANDY. I don't care what my mum said. She doesn't have to know. And if you tell her, I'll… I'll tell everyone why you're scared of going to sleep. Understand?

KATIE. You are kidding? Look, I was just trying to annoy you. I didn't mean it.

ANDY. I don't care.

KATIE. But it's dark outside! Andy, come back!!

ANDY *exits*.

Scene Eighteen

S is for Starlight

T is for Time

ANDY *is now outside. She looks up at the stars and wishes*.

ANDY.

Starlight, star bright,
First little star I see tonight,
Wish I may, wish I might
Have the first wish I wish tonight.

I wish I can find Radish. Please, please, *please*.

We hear a church clock striking twelve.

Music.

KATIE (*as she exits*). Auntie Carol!!

Scene Nineteen

U is for Under and Unconscious

As ANDY *journeys to Larkspur Lane, the rest of the* COMPANY *in sinister dark coats and hats, assemble the upturned table and chairs to form a tree, then exit*.

ANDY *crawls under the branches and falls asleep*.

Music fades.

Scene Twenty

V is for Visitor, Vanish and Vision

W is for Welcome

MRS PETERS *enters.* ANDY *wakes up and freezes.*

MRS PETERS. Hello? Hello? Is there anyone there? I'm sure I heard a noise…

MRS PETERS *exits to the side of the stage.*

We hear a car's brakes screech to a halt, followed by car doors slamming.

MUM (*off*). Simon, she's over here.

MUM *and* DAD *enter.*

Oh, Andy!

They both hug ANDY *and* DAD *puts his jacket around her.*

Thank goodness we've found you. Oh, Andy, darling, don't cry! It's all right, you're safe, we've got you. But why did you run away? We've been so *worried* –

DAD. We've been driving round all night looking for you!

MUM. But what on earth are you doing here in this garden?

ANDY. It's where I play.

DAD. In the middle of the night?!

ANDY. It's where I lost Radish. She's been so frightened without me. I had to come back and find her. She's just over there. If you put your arm down the tree, you can reach her. Please, Daddy.

DAD. That flaming rabbit!

MUM. But it's so early. We can't just barge into someone's garden. And you're frozen stiff. We ought to take you straight home, and I must tell Bill and the kids. They're all so worried. Katie's been in floods of tears.

ANDY. Katie?

DAD. Carrie and the twins were really upset too – not good with the baby so near.

ANDY. Oh, please, Dad?

DAD. We must ask permission.

ANDY. No, we can't. I'll get into trouble.

MRS PETERS *moves onstage.*

MUM. Oh! We're so sorry to disturb you like this – so early.

DAD. I know she's been very naughty playing in your garden, but my daughter's lost her toy rabbit around here somewhere. Do you mind if we have a look for it?

MRS PETERS. It's perfectly all right. She's our little visitor. She comes nearly every day and we're always so pleased to see her. Our grandchildren are all in Australia so we've no children of our own to come and play... Of course, we didn't want to intrude, but we couldn't help having little peeps now and then. You seemed to be having such fun. And yesterday you stayed such a long time we wondered if you'd like to come indoors and have some tea with us but when Arthur came out to ask, you ran away.

ANDY. I was scared. I'm sorry. Do you mind if my dad tries to get Radish back?

MRS PETERS. Not at all, my dear, although you can easily reach her yourself, you know. Why don't you go and look?

Music.

ANDY *inspects the tree and finds small items of furniture.*

That's upstairs. I think she's downstairs now. Round to the other side of the tree... Our daughter used to play with her dolls in this tree, and Arthur made her some furniture, so we put it all in there last night. Just our bit of fun.

ANDY. It's beautiful. So cosy. (*She finds the Radish doll.*) And here's Radish!! In her own little home. Oh, thank you, thank you!!

Music fades.

MRS PETERS. You're most welcome. Now, why don't you all come in and have a cup of tea? Arthur's put the kettle on.

MUM, DAD *and* MRS PETERS *exit.* GRAHAM *enters.*

ANDY. So, you see, it wasn't Radish's fault she fell down the tree, and it did all turn out okay in the end.

DAD (*off*). It's your fault. If only you'd looked after her properly when she went to bed...

MUM (*off*). What?! How can you say that when she doesn't even have a bed in your house...

ANDY. Well, almost... I know Mum and Dad will never get together again now. But I suppose it's all right.

Scene Twenty-One

X is for Xmas

Y is for Yacht

GRAHAM. And it's not the end yet. (*Exits.*)

ANDY. No, not yet. Because X marks the spot. And X is for... Xmas!!

ALL (*off*). Happy Christmas!

Carrie's home.

The TWINS *enter with a small home-made Christmas tree and a drawing.* ZEN *wears new boots and a Spiderman badge.* CRYSTAL *wears 'wobblies' on her head.*

CRYSTAL. This is for you, Andy. (*She gives* ANDY *a picture.*) I made it myself.

ANDY. It's beautiful. Really beautiful. Thank you, Crystal.

CRYSTAL (*shouting off*). Carrie, Andy said my picture is really beautiful. (*To* ANDY.) I stuck the sparkle on too, and the stars.

ZEN. Look at my new boots. They've got steel tips.

He kicks her.

DAD *and* CARRIE *enter wearing tinsel and carrying a wrapped-up present.*

DAD. Happy Christmas, Andy! (*He gives her the present.*)

ANDY. Oh, thanks, Dad.

CARRIE. It's from both of us.

ANDY (*opening the present*). A new suitcase! Wow. It's great!

CARRIE. Oooh... (*She clutches her stomach.*)

DAD. What's the matter?

CARRIE. Nothing. Just a twinge.

DAD. Perhaps you'd like a little drink of sherry?

CARRIE. Go on then, just a teeny one.

CARRIE *and* DAD *exit.*

CRYSTAL. Thanks for my wobblies, Andy. I love them.

ZEN. And my Spiderman badge. It's cool. (*As he exits.*) Carrie, I want a teeny sherry.

CRYSTAL (*as she exits*). Me too. What's sherry?

Mum's home.

PAULA *enters with a large decorated Christmas tree and gives* ANDY *a present.*

PAULA. Hi, Andy.

ANDY. For me?

ANDY *unwraps the present. It's a CD.*

PAULA. Some of my favourite tracks. Hope you like them.

ANDY. Wow! That's a great present. Thanks, Paula.

KATIE *enters and gives* ANDY *her present.* ANDY *unwraps an Andy Pandy doll.*

ANDY. Oh, an Andy Pandy doll. Thanks, Katie.

KATIE. And I've cleared half the windowsill for your things. So you can put it on there. Only half, remember?!

GRAHAM *enters and holds out his present. It is a beautiful toy yacht.*

ANDY. Wow – a yacht – Thanks, Graham. (*Reads the name on yacht.*) *HMS Britannia*. It's magnificent. You should show this to Mr Peters. Arthur loves woodwork.

BILL *and* MUM *enter wearing tinsel and blowing hooters, very merry.* BILL *hands* ANDY *a present.*

BILL. Here you are, darling, a nice big box of choccies.

MUM *gives* ANDY *her present – it's a handbag.*

MUM. Happy Christmas, darling.

ANDY. Thanks, Mum, it's cool.

Song – 'Unexpected Turns' Reprise

MUM.

Life can take some unexpected turns,
I can hardly believe it,
Everyone is here,
Graham, Katie, even dear old Paula –

BILL.

Hasn't she got taller, since we saw her last year?

GRAHAM.

But ring the bell, 'cos Andy's here as well!

ALL.

Life can take some unexpected turns,
Life can take some unexpected turns…

MUM (*speaking, as she exits*). I'll just put the turkey on.

BILL (*speaking, as he exits*). I'll help you with the stuffing.

PAULA (*speaking, as she exits*). I'm going to my room.

KATIE / GRAHAM / ANDY (*singing*).

Life can take some unexpected turns.

KATIE *exits*.

ANDY. In the end, it was an excellent Christmas.

GRAHAM. But it's not the end yet, Andy. Don't forget the alphabet. (*Exits*.)

ANDY. I won't, because my best, absolutely best present was –

Scene Twenty-Two

Z is for Zoë

Hospital.

DAD *enters with a bouquet of flowers and the* TWINS.

CARRIE *is wheeled on in a hospital bed. She is holding her new baby.*

DAD. Everyone ready? Here we go.

DAD, *the* TWINS *and* ANDY *approach the bed.*

DAD *and* CARRIE *kiss as he hands over the flowers.*

CARRIE. Thank you, darling, they're lovely. Hello, everyone.

ZEN. Yucky-yuck, do you have to do all that stupid kissin' stuff?

CRYSTAL. I want to see my sister.

CARRIE (*presents the baby*). Here she is. She's saying hello.

CRYSTAL. Can I hold her, please?

DAD. Maybe you're a bit little.

CRYSTAL. No, I'm not, am I, Mummy?

CARRIE. Come and sit on the bed and lean against me so that she can snuggle up.

The TWINS *are helped to climb onto the bed to cuddle the baby.*

CRYSTAL. Look at me, I'm holding my sister.

ZEN. I'm not big, I'm little, I'm a lickle wickle baby.

CARRIE. Come here, little baby.

ANDY *gets out her Radish doll.* DAD *notices.*

DAD. Do you want to hold your sister too, Andy?

ANDY. No, thanks. I'm not really bothered about babies.

CARRIE. Why don't you have a turn? You might be able to stop her crying.

ANDY. There's no room on the bed.

CARRIE. Well, you're big enough to hold her properly.

ANDY *takes the baby and holds her.*

Music.

ANDY *is entranced.*

ANDY. She's holding my hand.

DAD. She likes you. She's stopped crying.

ANDY. She's so little.

CARRIE. She's actually quite big for a baby, much stronger and longer than Zen and Crystal were. I think she's going to be tall.

ANDY. Like me.

DAD. Well, she is your sister, so it's not really surprising.

CARRIE. Is she still going to be called Ethel?

ZEN. Ethel? Yucky!

ANDY. No, it's a stupid name. She's so pretty, she ought to have a pretty name.

DAD. Well, what do you reckon? We've got A for Andy and C for Crystal. What about B for…

ZEN. Belly-button!

ANDY. But, if you have a B, you might have a D and an E and an F and… What about a Z name?

ZEN. Yeah, Z's the best. Z for Zen. Yo!

ANDY. Okay, then how about Z for…

Music fades.

Zoë.

CARRIE *and* DAD *nod in agreement and smile.*

ANDY *hands* BABY ZOË *back. Hugs all round.*

ANDY. So, Radish and me, we're okay now. I've got a House A and a House B, but I've got a House C too. I go to Mum's one week, to see Graham and Katie, and Dad's the next, where I get to play with my little sister Zoë. But I go to Mr and Mrs Peters nearly every day to play with Radish, though she still lives in my pocket most of the time.

It takes a lot of organising. But it's all right. I've got it sorted now.

It's as easy as A, B, C.

Really.

Music. The other actors, with the puppets, enter.

Song – 'Unexpected Turns' Reprise

ALL.

Life can take some unexpected turns,
Suddenly you're heading down a different path,
When you're not looking it will come and find you,
Sneak up behind you just to have a laugh.

As a wise man once said,
Before he lost his head,
Life can take some unexpected turns,
Life can take some unexpected turns,
Life can take some unexpected turns.

Lights fade.

Blackout.

The End.